A Planetary
Acceptance

by Simonne Murphy
Illustrations by Molly Sullivan

A Planetary Fairytale
Acceptance

by Simonne Murphy

Cover and illustrations by Molly Sullivan

International Standard Book Number
978-1-934976-60-9

Published by ACS Publications
an imprint of Starcrafts LLC
334-A Calef Highway, Epping, NH 03042

http://www.astrocom.com
http://www.acspublications.com
http://www.starcraftspublishing.com

This book is dedicated
to all my children and
granchildren.
Love you!

Mommy, Grammy,
Memere

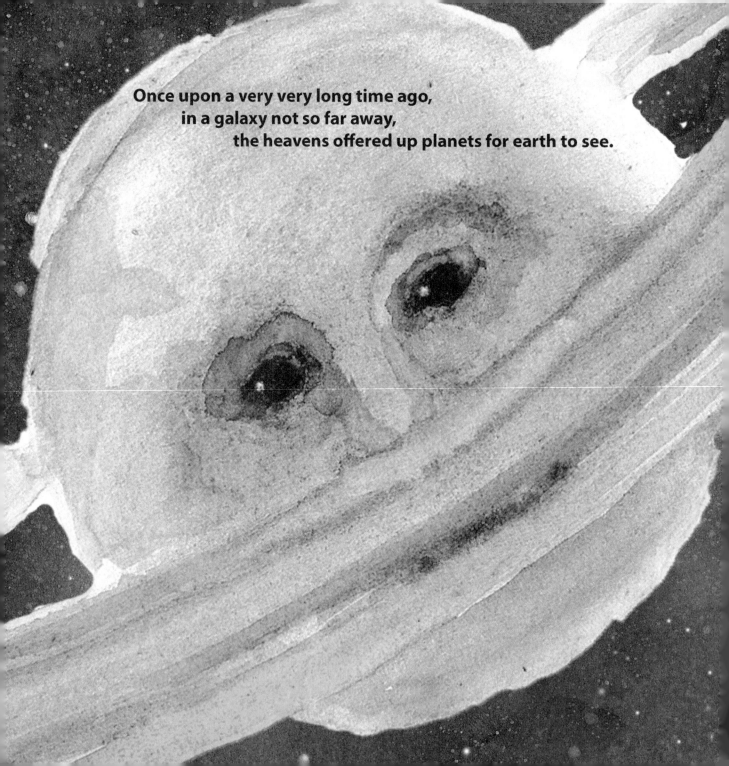

Once upon a very very long time ago,
in a galaxy not so far away,
the heavens offered up planets for earth to see.

Some were BIG planets like Saturn
and some were not so big like Mercury, Mars and Venus.

All the planets got along, orbiting the Sun and playing hide and seek with the Moon.

The Sun is the big guy, who brightens up everyone's day.
The Sun is also the king, and try as he might, he cannot seem to keep
all the others in order—they sometimes try to go their own way.

The Moon is the night light, keeping watch over all the others as the Sun sleeps. The Moon did not like hurt feelings. She wanted all the planets to get along.

Sometimes Moon seems to light up the whole night sky, so it's easier for her to keep watch.

Other times she hides part of herself,
just to keep them guessing who she's watching.

The planets orbit and play games with each other.
Saturn is big on ring games, trying to catch things in its rings.
Mars wants to paint everything, and that means everything, red.
Jupiter likes racing around and challenging others to races.

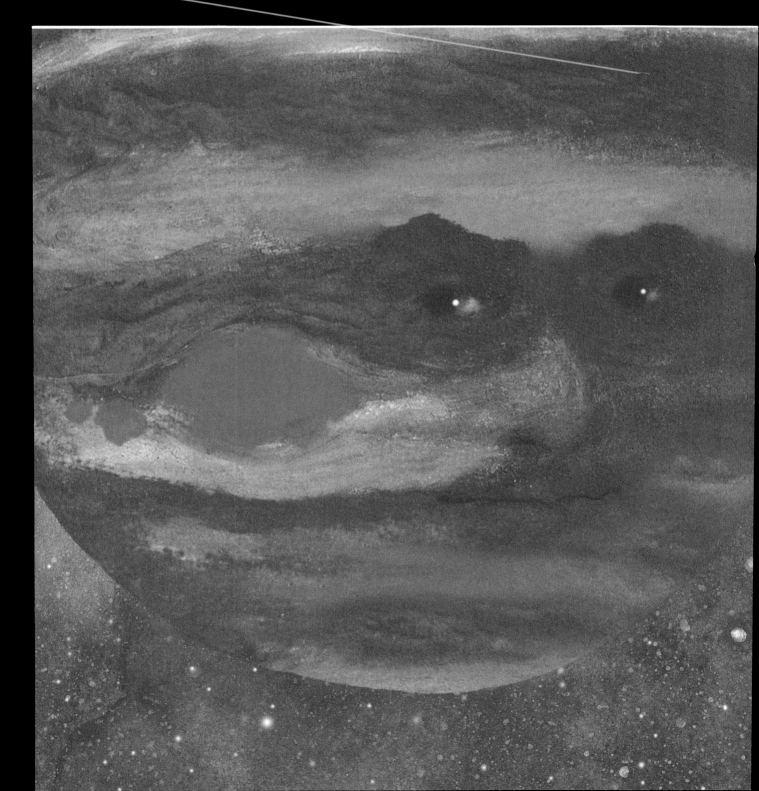

But there are some little planets,
hidden from view ...

but all too ready to be part of the family.

They are Ceres and Eris.

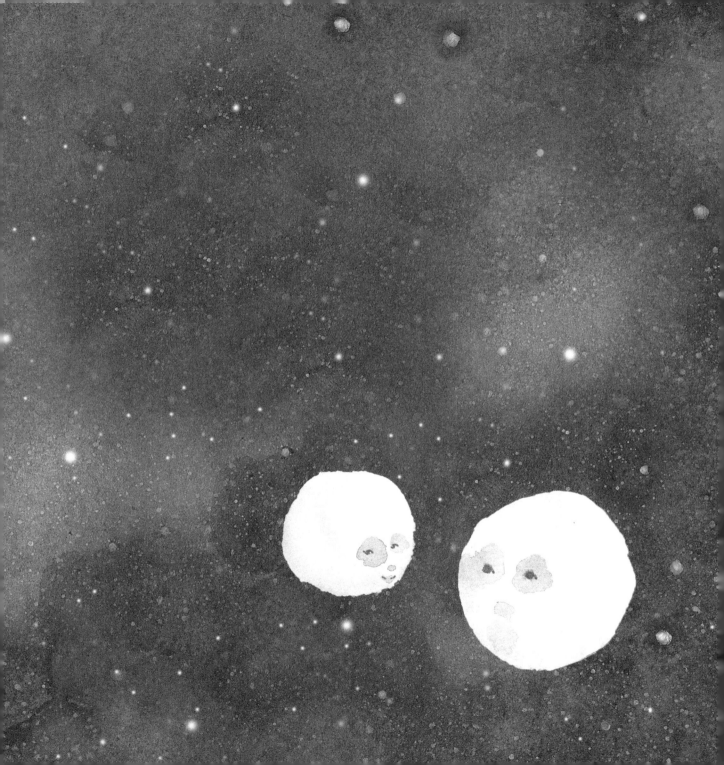

Now the bigger planets did not want to let these little planets play in the same galaxy, so they said,

"You are too small! No one will notice you!

You are not as important as we big planets."

The little planets puffed themselves up as big as they could.
They knew that the heavens wanted them there—

they had a purpose!

Mercury said, "I don't want to deal with this right now.
Let's just not even talk about it."

"Why should we worry about them?" said Saturn.
"Really, we're the ones who matter."

"Why don't we just push them out of the way and be done
with it!" shouted Mars. "I agree with Saturn that we're more
important then those little pests will ever be."

"They're not even as beautiful as we are" said Venus." Look at how we
bigger planets just make the galaxy so much more! Ditch those others
and lets move on."

"This is making me too sad!" exclaimed Jupiter. "Are you sure we're
doing the right thing? What if it doesn't work out?"

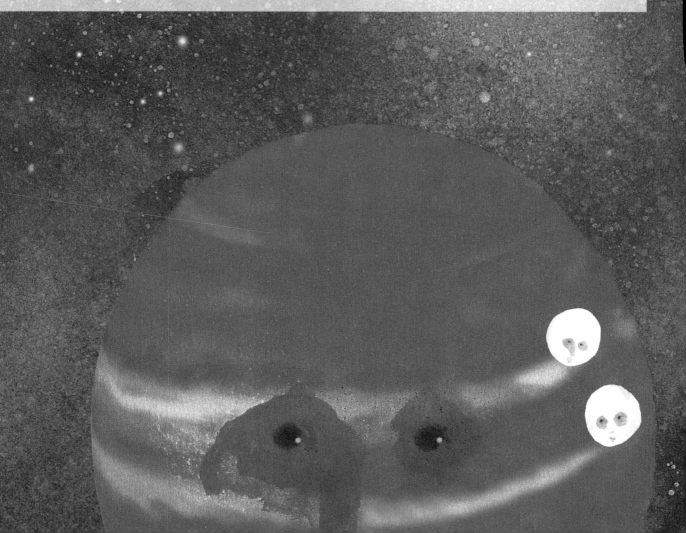

"I'm going to do what I want to do!" shouted Uranus.
" What is wrong with the rest of you? You are all a bunch of sissys!"

Neptune didn't know what to say.
"Maybe they'll think that of me next!" he thought.

"Oh my!" said Mercury. He was so stunned that he stopped right where he was.
"I guess maybe I should stop and think about this. Venus said the small planets
might be valuable. "Maybe they will bring more love and joy to our galaxy."

Earth was puzzled. "I'm staying out of this!
I have enough problems dealing with humans!"

Mars looked at the others and wondered about their own desires.
"Are you all thinking about what's in it for you?"

Jupiter wasn't having any of it. "Well, we are important and so much bigger than those little planets but maybe we should all get along and give them a chance! "

Jupiter, the largest of the planets, who was spinning so fast that it made the others dizzy, always tried to take up as much space as possible in the night sky.

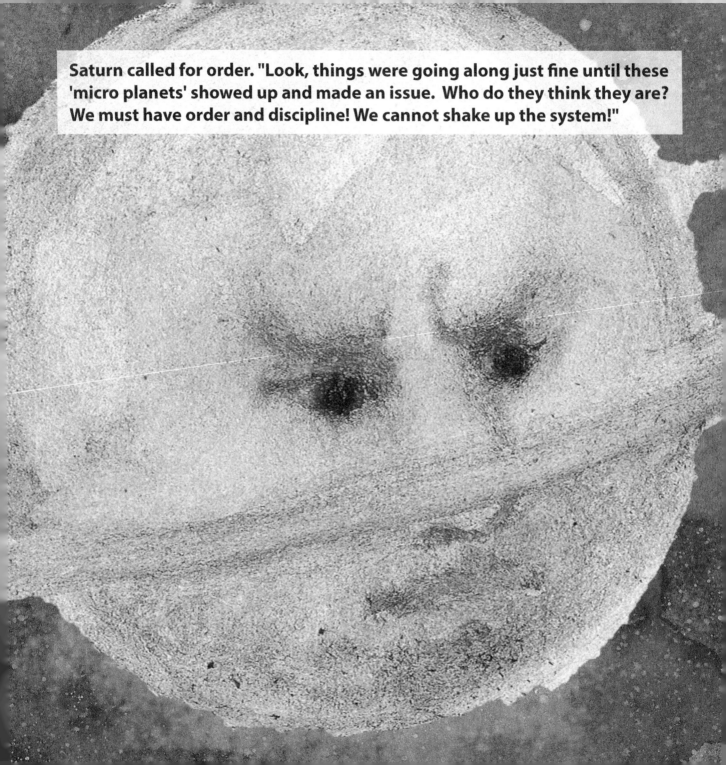

Saturn called for order. "Look, things were going along just fine until these 'micro planets' showed up and made an issue. Who do they think they are? We must have order and discipline! We cannot shake up the system!"

Uranus was up next. "Well, I was a newbie once too. We are all individuals and all have something unique to offer. Maybe we should give them a chance. I've learned to get along with Saturn—we make meaningful changes."

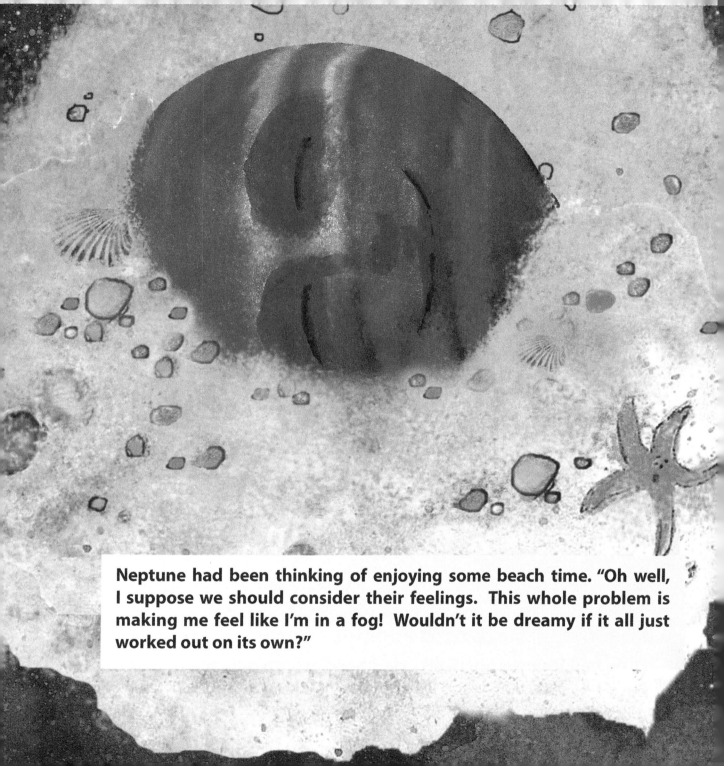

Neptune had been thinking of enjoying some beach time. "Oh well, I suppose we should consider their feelings. This whole problem is making me feel like I'm in a fog! Wouldn't it be dreamy if it all just worked out on its own?"

Pluto had his own problems. He'd been accepted by the bigger planets until the upstarts, Eris and Ceres, started making noise about themselves.

Pluto could be a little on the dark side, but the final transformations are beautiful! He commented,

"Let's just get this all out in the open and be done with it! Better days are coming! Let's clear the air!"

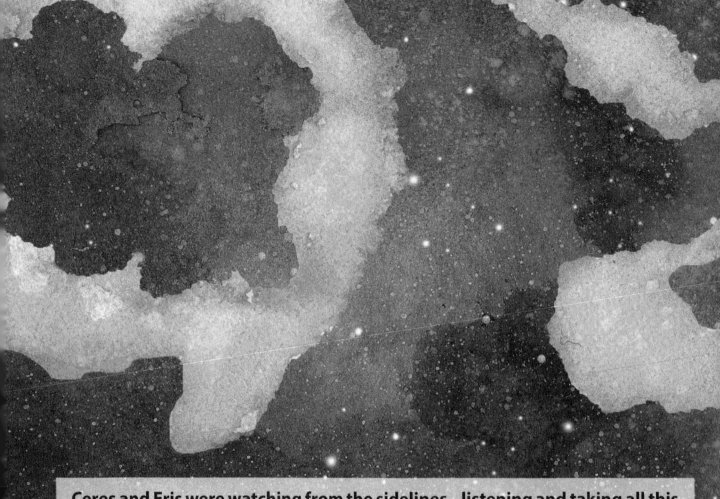

Ceres and Eris were watching from the sidelines...listening and taking all this

Eris, not one big who was big on sharing and had been remaining quietly on the sidelines, was disgusted, so she said, "Oh please! This is not some beauty or popularity contest!   Not one of you is perfect by any means."

Ceres tried to keep the peace. "Now we must all get along as the Sun says. I'll tell you what, why don't we all try to love and nurture each other! We can make the universe a better place to live!"

Yes, each had tried to come up with a solution but there still wasn't one.

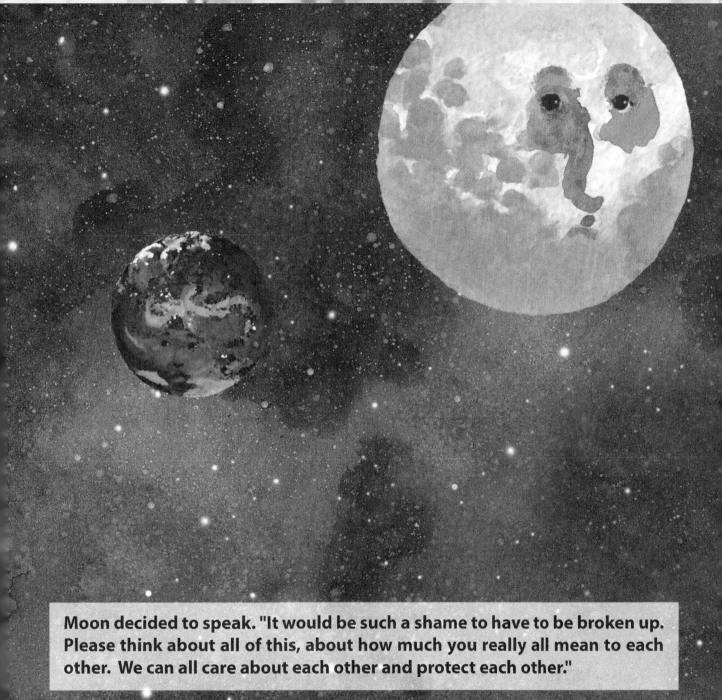

Moon decided to speak. "It would be such a shame to have to be broken up. Please think about all of this, about how much you really all mean to each other. We can all care about each other and protect each other."

Mercury spoke up. "If we really try, we can learn to communicate. We're all intelligent and can be rational, if we put our minds to it. We can all get along."

"Well said," the Sun commented. "Mercury, you can stay."

"Wait!" said Venus. "I had a thought also. We all have our own graceful beauty which is only made better by being with each other. I think it would be a shame if one or more of us went away!"

"I think you have the idea, Venus," said the Sun. "You, too, can stay."

The rest of the planets were still, as they pondered their situation.

They knew the Sun would let them stay, if they promised to get along.

"I like to be independent!" said Mars, "You all know that. I'd stick up for any of you and your rights—even the new little planets.
Everyone needs a place to belong."

"Hoorah Mars!" said the Sun. 'I believe you have the idea. You too can stay."

"You are all right," sighed Jupiter. "We've been bullies to the little planets and I'd like to say I'm sorry.

Eris and Ceres, if you can forgive us, then welcome to the family!"

Saturn was next. "We're very sorry little planets. We need to learn some discipline and learn about you. We have not been fair and we too were once waiting to be accepted."

The Sun thought to himself, "I believe they might all come to their senses.

During all of this Pluto, Eris and Ceres had been almost hiding behind the Sun. This was a new concept for them. Pluto, had to re-fight his way back into the group.

Eris smirked and had to control herself not to start throwing apples. Ceres was patiently and silently watching it all.

"I say let's give it a chance!" shouted Uranus. "We can't let things like size be the deciding thing. Sometimes being smaller is best, and we have yet to even know how we can help each other. I know I'd be lost without Saturn to keep me in check. Thanks for that , by the way , Saturn!"

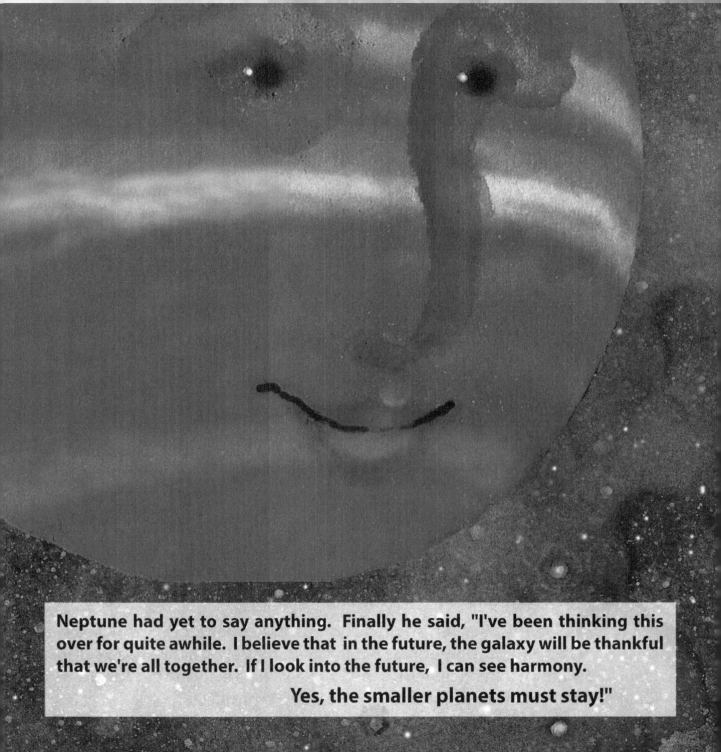

Neptune had yet to say anything. Finally he said, "I've been thinking this over for quite awhile. I believe that in the future, the galaxy will be thankful that we're all together. If I look into the future, I can see harmony.

Yes, the smaller planets must stay!"

"Well, well!" said the Sun. You have all made your points, and I've decided you can all stay. But first, we need to hear from our smaller planets, and Pluto should be the first to speak.

"Sometimes things have to change to make way for the new" said Pluto. "Our differences had to be set aside. I want you to know, even though I'm not a very big in size, I am big enough to help you all through the healing and the renewing. I also want you to know that I used to be bigger."

The planets could not help but smile at Pluto.
He was one little guy with a BIG heart.

Eris could not wait to speak. "It is rumored that all I want is discord and disharmony. Okay, so I do get a kick out of a good fight or squabble. I can also be pretty understanding...just not when you'd normally expect it. Thanks for giving me a chance."

Ceres was beaming. "I am so happy that we'll all be one big happy family! Tell you what, you're all invited over for dinner! Bring the family. Oh this makes me so very happy!"

All was right in the galaxy, once again!

About the Author—Simonne Murphy

Simonne Murphy is the one on the staff of Starcrafts LLC and Astro Computing Services who always knows where everything is and how to fix it, even when (or maybe especially when the principal (owner) is frustrated. Simonne is addicted to books (she was once a librarian) and is a primary editor and profreader for all we publish. *A Planetary Fairytale* is the second book she has written for us. The first one was *Ceres*, written just after asteroid Ceres was promoted to planet in 2006. But now that she's gotten off the ground as a writer, Simonne has also written two more "Fairytales, and she writes "Airspace" for our newsletter, too!

About the Illustrator—Molly Sullivan

Molly received her Bachelor of Fine Arts degree from Ringling School of Art. She is an active member of Seacoast Art Association and a regular exhibitor of her fine art work at the SAA and other galleries.

She is on our staff at Starcrafts LLC, where her special talents in art and art production are significant for the publishing part of our business. Molly will have more art projects ahead!

Molly's eight year old daughter, Reilly, also deserves mention here, since she has served as a prime critic and advisor for this "Planetary Fairytale" project!

A Planetary
Fairytale #2
will be
Coming Soon!
This one
will be about
Friendship

Sun, Moon and all of the planets in our solar system will return again, and this time the story and their conversation will reveal how they handle relationships. You'll learn how some of them get along with each other quite naturally, while others have some differences that don't always blend that well.

And. . . there will be more! The next one is:
A Planetary Fairytale — Patience

Astro Computing Services
ACS Publications & Starcrafts Publishing
Your best source for everything in astrology!

Easy to Use Software!

Personalized Astrology Lessons

These lessons offer you an opportunity to master the age-old discipline of astrology with your own chart as your primary example. The lessons were designed by Maritha Pottenger to help curious beginners understand all the tools that astrology has to offer. You'll reinforce these lessons with a "homework" assignments that test your knowledge! Have your birth date, time and location ready when you place your order.

32 lessons on one order with notebook—$105.95

Any 6 lessons on one chart—$27.95

One lesson —$6.95   Notebook only— $8.95

The Electronic Astologer Software

~~he four software packages shown at right are for Windows, XP, Vista or 7. They
~~ude the full ACS Atlas database and are very easy to use—no prior knowl-
~ of astrology is needed. You can calculate a horoscope for anyone for whom
~ve birth date, time and place. Then you can view or print the chart and
~comprehensive text report about it.

~ Your Horoscope" allows you to easily produce and print a natal chart
~ interpretation of it.

~Your Future " software enables you to produce secondary progressed
~calculations and print extensive text reports.

~ur Romance" software allows you to compare any two horocopes,
~heet that rates the partners for attraction, love, sexual sizzle and
~Etensive interpreted reports.

~is $74.95 OR you can buy the "All Three" program for $175.

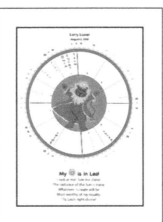

9 781934 976609